Christmas

on Concourse C

a Place to Belong book

By Megan Meredith

A place to belong book: Christmas on Concourse C

Megaphone Publishing Ltd. Co.

Cover Design by KMR Designs

Editing by HG editing

A massive winter storm catches most of the country off guard. On Christmas Eve. In Nashville, a group of strangers will be brought together by nature and by a handsome man with mysterious generosity.

Strangers can become friends in a matter of hours, but what will surprise Blake, a research analyst, who was reluctantly on her way home for Christmas, is that they can become like family.

IBSN: 9798362982607

To Hallmark. Big Mistake.

Chapter 1

"Folks," a midwestern female voice started as the intercom crackled, "I do apologize. We are waiting on further information, but it looks like Flight 8752 to Boston as well as all other flights in or out tonight have been cancelled at this time."

What she said after that was drowned out by the murmurings, cuss words, and furious exclamations that rose like a wave through the four gates interconnected at the end of Concourse C. I watched the woman's mouth continue to move behind the counter but could not hear the words. Something about blizzard conditions. But soon, the desk was so swarmed with disgruntled passengers that I could no longer even see her. The poor airline employee was swallowed up in holiday fury even though she had no control over the pilots, the flights, or, *for heaven's sake*, the weather.

Hell hath no fury like those stranded in an airport, I thought to myself, which made my shoulders shake with involuntary laughter. I quickly smothered my amusement, knowing I'd have to call my parents with the bad news, but I opted to wait, prolonging their disappointment and my discomfort.

Maybe dinner is warranted first. With everyone fighting with desperation—*and in vain*, I thought —to get home for Christmas, there was surely no one in the cafes or the food court. I wandered lazily through several gates and concourses before I found a chain restaurant that I liked simply because it looked and smelled like a French bistro.

"No mad dashes, miss?" A red-haired waitress smiled at me, handing me a menu. "Taking a break for dinner? Smart," she commented as she tucked a pen behind her ear. "What'll ya have?"

"No point in it. If I can't get out of here, I certainly can't get in to Massachusetts. By land, air, or sea...," I said rather dryly as I looked over the menu. "I'll have the—" But before I could finish, I was interrupted by a lanky fellow in a dashing suit, who slid over from the bar, craning over to my booth. "I'm so sorry," he apologized with a British accent. "I couldn't help but hear—it sounded like you said the flights have been cancelled?"

He'd obviously been too busy drinking and watching the "*tele*," I mimicked in my head, to have heard the announcements.

"I'm pretty sure *all* the flights out have been cancelled," Blake announced with slight uncertainty. The lanky British man let out a series of curse words that somehow didn't sound so offensive when expertly strung together with his accent.

"Thank you. I am so sorry to interrupt," he said as he laid cash next to his beer and gathered his coat and duffle. "And for my language. Please excuse me," he apologized as he scurried off, already shouting into his phone, his elegant accent trailing off into nothing as he ran further down the concourse. I raised my eyebrows and smiled at the waitress.

"I'll have the French dip, please."

"It's a good day for that, hun. I'll have that right out. You drinking tonight?"

I chuckled. "Not yet."

The waitress scribbled something on a pad and chuckled herself as she whisked away, stopping at the farthest booth and patting a broad shoulder that barely peeked out from behind the leather booth before she disappeared into the kitchen. The broad shoulder turned slightly, and a head of dark hair, thick brows over dark eyes glanced my way. I sort of nodded in an awkward acknowledgment but wondered why he was looking over. But that was my natural tendency—to wonder why people were being kind to me, paying attention to me, talking to me, or even noticing me.

I took a sip of my water and remembered looking in the mirror before leaving my apartment today and thinking that it was as good as it would get. Which is my usual attitude toward my thick, wavy yet mousy brown hair, my sporadic freckles, and my not entirely crooked but not entirely symmetrical nose. I wasn't ugly...I didn't think. At least I'd never been told that. But I wasn't entirely sure I was what one would call eye-catching. And, though research was my bread and butter, I had no idea what a person needed in order to be so. I had a boy's name, and sometimes, people like that end up being strikingly gorgeous, causing a sort of attractive juxtaposition. Not with me, though.

I caught people off guard, because they expected to see a boy when they called the name Blake, and then they would give me this look like they felt sorry for me. Even still, I tended to fly under the radar and blend in to the wallpaper (preferably plaid or floral), and, at this point in my life, I was okay with that. As an art and history researcher, being invisible was, honestly, one of things I was best at.

Broad-Shoulders' turning probably meant nothing. The waitress had probably said, "There's a lonely one over there," and he'd wanted to gawk at the sad spectacle in the front booth. But I couldn't help the flush that rose up my neck as a shy smirk hooked at the edge of his mouth in response to my awkward nod. I quickly ducked my head and studied the dessert menu even though I had no intention of ordering any.

It is Christmas Eve, Blake, I scolded myself. *And you are stranded in an airport. Have some pie, dammit.*

Soon, my sandwich arrived, and I was thankful because it gave me something else to think about. While I studied the steam coming off the au jus and the grain in the roast beef, I wondered how to sound disappointed that I wasn't going to make it when I called my parents. I planned the conversation out in my head. I would call; Dad would answer most likely, because Mom was always elbow-deep in baking by now. He would be his level of excited to hear my voice on the phone, but there would be a vacancy in his tone partially because he had no idea how to talk to me and partially because there was a game on. Mother would be heard in the background barking at him to hang on and keep talking to me while she cleaned her hands or wiped the counter or something, but, inevitably, he would just lay the phone down on the counter and walk away. Mom would start shouting at the phone, telling me not to hang up and that she was coming, and, eventually, she'd pick up the phone and be out of breath from all the scurrying. I'd explain about the snowstorm that had hit and the winds. I'd go on to explain that planes further north couldn't get here, and the ice and snow that were coming in thick now were making it impossible to get out. I was stranded in my layover and wouldn't be home for Christmas. She would begin to cry and then somehow find a way to make me feel guilty for getting stranded, like I'd picked too late of a flight or I should have paid attention to weather better or I should never have moved away in the first place. I would try to remain calm and do the best I could to placate to her, but, on the inside, I would be seething that she was making this even remotely my fault. She would ask me a bunch of questions like where would I stay and who I was with and if I had pepper spray. Eventually, I would find an excuse to get off the phone and promise to check in later. And that would be that. I wasn't coming home for Christmas.

As the bread soaked up the savory steaming liquid, I decide to put the whole thing off till later.

Chapter 2

No longer feeling the need to stay close to my gate, I wandered around my terminal for an hour or so after finishing my supper, looking in the shops before parking myself in front on a series of couches arranged in front of a Christmas tree that had to be a hundred feet tall, sitting just at the opening of Concourse C.

The couches were sleek, modern, and a deep navy blue that matched almost every airline's logo in some way. They were arranged in a U-shape at the base of the tree, which was expertly decorated with enormous gold balls, large globe ornaments, and every variation of plane ornament one could possibly imagine. The swirls of ribbon and tinsel were all evenly puffed and spaced, cascading down and around the tree like a fountain of air travel cheer. And I couldn't help but think about who's job that was. *Do they only work once a year? Do they get calls from famous airports and hotels to come decorate their trees? Did they get referrals because someone had seen their work at JFK or Heathrow? How much did they get paid to decorate a Christmas tree at an airport?*

It didn't much matter, though it was amusing to think about, and, truth be told, I was just stalling. No doubt Dad would see the cancellations on the news and alert Mom, and soon enough, they'd be calling me, upset that they hadn't heard it from me. So, it was better to head them off and call them. I got my phone out and dialed their house phone—they still had a landline and could rarely find their cell phones in time to answer them before they quit ringing.

"Hey, Dad," I said as he answered the phone louder than necessary.

"Honey, it's Blake," Dad announced to Mom across the house before even speaking to me. "Is your flight in?"

"Uh, no, Dad." I shifted against the navy blue cushion, wishing this was already over. "All the flights have been cancelled. I'm actually stranded in Nashville."

"Oh. Well, what's the weather doing? Let's see here...." I could hear him changing the channels and then listening to the weather reports being updated. Lots of airports shut down, flights cancelled in several states because of the ice storm and snow that was moving in across most of the country. I hadn't told him all that, but now, he couldn't argue with me about it; he'd heard it on the news for himself. But I knew what was coming. "Should have gotten an earlier flight."

"Yes, well, I don't think anyone was prepared for the severity of this storm. And I had to work. I got out as soon as I could." I defended myself pointlessly and sucked on my teeth so I wouldn't huff loudly into the phone.

"Can't rent a car then, I suppose?"

"No, I'm pretty sure they are shutting everything down. The road conditions are really bad. Plus, even if I drove all night, I still wouldn't make it to Massachusetts for Christmas."

"Alright, well, here's your mother," he said abruptly as he laid the phone down.

I closed my eyes, swallowing the frustration and seething that I felt at the moment and doing my very best to muster a perky voice to repeat the conversation with Mom. I could hear her sniffing before she even answered the phone, and I assumed she was already crying. I took another deep breath as I opened my eyes. But what I saw as I did stole my exhale and the words I was about to say to Mom.

Isn't that the same dark hair? I only saw his eyes for a split second and that shy smirk—but aren't they the exact same? He sat down at the edge of one of the couches that made the side of the U and studied the tree.

"Blake?" Mom said in a way that made me think she'd said it once already. I made a throaty noise into the phone that probably sounded like a frog, but my confusion had frozen my tongue to the roof of my mouth. *It's not really a small airport, so what are the odds that he'd come sit down in front of the same tree as me after we just sat in the same cafe and awkwardly acknowledged each other?* I squinted at him, though he hadn't even looked my way at all—*as if that would help me understand why he chose to sit here.* I inwardly rolled my eyes at myself.

"Blake, honey, I just saw the weather." Mom's voice drew me away from my analysis of the dark stranger, and I ducked my head away from him, hoping I hadn't been too obvious. I supposed I could just get up and walk away, but, selfishly, I didn't want to leave my spot. *I was here first,* I thought in a completely mature way.

"Hey, Mom. Yeah, looks like I won't make it home for Christmas."

"I know, sweetie—I just saw the news. I'm so sorry." I could hear her rustling about the kitchen as she spoke, a lid on a pot, the oven door closing, the kettle whistling, and, finally, her hands against her towel, which she threw over her shoulder. "I wish you could have gotten a flight out earlier."

"Me too, Mom. Sorry I can't make it," I forced myself to say, but I stopped myself from saying more.

"Are you going to be okay there? Will they put you up in a hotel? Are you safe? Do you have enough money? Oh, sweetie, you're alone on Christmas. This is why I wish you hadn't moved." She somehow managed to fuss over me and shame me at the same time.

"I'm pretty sure the hotels are full, Mom; the entire airport is stranded here. But everything will be fine, okay? I'm just sorry I can't be there for Christmas." I forced it out again.

"Okay. Well. Call us later, okay? Check in?" she worried.

"Okay, Mom. Tell Dad I said Merry Christmas."

And with that, it was over.

Sliding the phone back into my purse, I wanted to slump down onto the couch—and I would have if the dark-haired man wasn't sitting adjacent to me. Instead, I propped my head up with my arm on the back of the couch and stared at the tree, listening to the Christmas music over the speakers. I would love to be home—*my home*, I thought—in front of my fireplace with a cup of hot coffee. But I supposed there were worse ways to spend Christmas Eve. I at least had found a comfortable spot in front of Christmas lights.

The dark-haired, broad man glanced my way and smiled the same shy smile that he had in the cafe. Then, he slid over to the end of his couch nearer to me.

"I promise I'm not following you," he said. "I came to sit in front of this tree, and then I recognized you from the cafe after I sat down. Now, I feel like I should introduce myself."

I laughed a little awkwardly and tucked my hair behind my ear. He half-stood and leaned toward me, extending a hand.

"I'm Nick."

"Blake," I said shaking his hand. I noticed his brows arced just slightly, as most people's did when I told them my name.

He sat back down. "Nice to meet you, Blake."

"Nice to meet you too."

"Trying to get home for Christmas?" he asked, crossing his legs out long in front of him.

"I was trying to get to my parents'," I clarified and then wondered why I'd felt the need to do that.

"I see. I wasn't trying to eavesdrop, but I couldn't help but overhear, and I do think they are giving out lots of hotel vouchers."

"Oh, I know. I just figured there's tons of families and elderly people who could use a bed more than I could. I don't mind adventure sleeping."

He nodded thoughtfully and looked out toward the windows. "Wow, it's really getting nasty out there."

"Yep," I agreed as several families passed by with kids and suitcases in tow.

"So many stressed-out people today," he observed. His voice almost sounded like he was taking responsibility for it.

"Yeah, I can't imagine dealing with this with a family."

"I hear the airport is taking good care of everyone with small children."

"Oh?" I said, wondering how he knew that. Several girls passed by with not more than crop tops and high heels on. I subdued a scoff, but Nick commented what we must have both been thinking.

"I just wish some had dressed appropriately for winter. Maybe we should offer them something from the lost and found." He smirked at me, and I had to work hard not to snort with laughter as I watched the girls sashay down the concourse.

"People are funny," I said.

"They are. I saw several fights breaking out already. You'd think people could be kind in situations like this. Knowing there's nothing to be done until the weather clears."

"Seems too much to ask for such an underdeveloped species," I said sarcastically.

A musician set his guitar down by the tree and lay down near it, using the case as a pillow. We both laughed a little at that, maybe because the other side of the couch was not taken, and he could have had something soft to lay on but chose the ground and the hard plastic case. Maybe it wasn't about the quality of sleep; maybe it was about not getting the instrument stolen while he slept, Nick pointed out. I nodded at his estimate, and we continued to comment on the various shapes and sizes of the mostly angry people we saw pass by. After a while, we gradually fell silent, watching the ice and snow fall in harrowing thick curtains outside.

After a few moments, he stood. "I am missing my fireplace right about now. I'm going in search of something else warm. Want a coffee too?"

Hadn't I just thought that? Surely I didn't say it out loud.... "No, I'm good, thanks," I said even though I did want a frothy milk, cinnamon, and whipped cream. I wanted Christmas in a cup, but I didn't want to say that to this stranger who had just offered to buy me a drink. No one had ever done that before. What did it mean?

"Alright. Save my spot though?" He laughed and walked away before I could answer anything.

Now is the perfect time to disappear. I was sure I could find another tree in some other terminal to sit by and stare at. But just as I looped the strap of my purse on my shoulder and was going to stand up and venture off, three young Asian women sat down next to me. I broadly assumed they were exchange students coming or going on their holiday.

"We are going to play this game. Do you want to play with us? We need a fourth."

The surprise on my face must have exceeded what I intended, because one of the girls giggled, and the other two began talking overtop of each other in rapid succession.

"You are by yourself, no? You can play with us?" the one that had giggle asked innocently.

It was a strategy game about settlers. I had played it before and was mostly bad at it, but I honestly had nothing else to do—I was indeed by myself—and their faces were so eager, so "Yes, I can play with you" came out of my mouth.

No disappearing now.

Chapter 3

As I checked my watch, a groan formed in my throat. Only ten minutes had passed since we'd started playing this game. I remembered it being a long game, but this was going to take forever with these three. I had conquered most of the territory and hoarded all the resources I could, but it was still dragging on when Nick reappeared with two cups of coffee. I tried my hardest not to look up at him when he sat down, but a brief glance at him caught the flicker of surprise in his eyes.

"They messed up my order. Do you want this one?" he stated as he extended the cup to me. *What are the odds,* I thought. *I wanted coffee, didn't ask for it, and they messed one up with this guy, who I told I didn't want one?*

"It has cinnamon and whipped cream, though. You may not like it. I prefer nutmeg."

The students began giggling again, and I suspected my face was betraying me. *Seriously? It has cinnamon and whipped cream?* Was this guy telepathic? The odds are not in my favor, and I am not lucky, like, ever.

He leaned over a little closer and whispered, "You don't have to take it if you don't want to." I knew he was whispering because I had created the most awkward scene, staring blankly at the cup and at him without any indication of whether or not I would take the cup he was holding in midair for me.

"I'm so sorry," I said, shaking my head and taking the cup, our fingers brushing as we made the exchange. "It's just that I was wishing for one of these almost specifically, and it's a little strange that they messed up your order, basically giving me what I wanted."

He laughed a little and settled back into his spot on the couch, taking a sip from his coffee *with nutmeg*, and nodded toward the game. "What are ya'll playing here?"

The three students looked up in surprise and began giggling again but didn't speak to him.

"It's Settlers," I answered, adding my final pieces, effectively cutting off the rest and winning the game. "And I just won."

The giggling continued as the others clapped a little and cleaned up the game. "We go find another game and come back, okay?"

I smiled at them and nodded. "Okay." They scurried off, and I was again alone in front of the tree with Nick.

"That was kind of you." He said it in a way that sounded condescending or brotherly, but his face held that same timid expression that he'd had before.

I shrugged awkwardly, wondering whether to say thank you or not, but, after I took a sip from my Christmas cup, I realized it was too late, so I let my awkward shrug just hang there. *Gosh, the coffee is perfect*, I thought. *When everything else is wrong, at least something is right.*

I stared at the tree and listened to the bustle of the airport all around me when the thought scurried across my mind: *I have effectively disappeared.* As I sipped on my coffee, I smiled behind my cup.

"What?" Nick asked from his couch, crossing his legs in front of him again and leaning back heavily into the couch.

"Oh—what?" I hadn't realized he could see my smile or would care to know. "Nothing." I tried to play it off. "I just..." I trailed off.

"No, it's cool. I'm a stranger." He laughed. "You don't have to tell me. You just had a bit of a conniving smile, and I wondered what was behind it."

Was it possible to have a shy, timid smile but be really outgoing? This stranger was, in fact, very strange to me.

"I thought about trying to disappear earlier," I admitted, "but I just realized I already had. I'm in an overly crowded airport where no one knows me."

"Why would you want to disappear?" Nick asked.

I choked a little on my coffee, surprised that this conversation was continuing. I would have thought my answer would have been sufficient and was shocked that it wasn't.

"Oh! It's not that I want to per se," I said, emphasizing "want." "It's more like...a hidden talent? I'm just pretty good at it."

Nick made some sort of "hmm" noise and squinted at me slightly before asking, "So, where do your parents live?"

Now we were back on familiar small-talk territory. "Massachusetts."

"Might as well be the frozen tundra this year. Harsh winter, huh?"

I nodded, remembering the bitterness of the cold as a child, how it could pierce your skin and bite at your bones even through layers upon layers.

"What about you?" I asked. "Where were you headed?"

He ran his hands through his dark bristly hair and clasped them behind his head. "I am a bit of a nomad, I'm afraid. I was headed to the East Coast for a job."

"Will this storm set you back?" I asked, wondering why I was still engaging in conversation.

"Nah. I was headed to some friends' to spend Christmas with them. Job won't kick off till after the new year."

"That's nice," I said without thinking but then retracted. "About having a break before the job begins. Not about missing Christmas with your friends."

He nodded as if he had known what I had meant, took a sip from his coffee, and then leaned out far on his knees. "So, I guess you've got family waiting for you," he asked, and I saw his eyes drop lightning fast to my hands and back up. *Did he just check for a wedding band?*

My cheeks flushed at the realization, and I took a sip of coffee out of habit, trying desperately to hide behind the cup.

"Uh, not exactly. Heading to my parents for Christmas is more of an obligation. I doubt either of us will miss it." I almost added that I didn't have my own family, but I held my tongue, knowing he had already seen I wasn't married. I assumed at that moment that his phone must have buzzed in his pocket by the way it shocked him and he jolted a little, setting his cup down and sliding the phone from his pocket.

"Speak of the devil," he said. He excused himself and walked to the far window to have his conversation, in which I assumed he was letting his friend down easy about not being able to make it for Christmas and that, based on the fury of the storm, he'd be more than a day late.

I surveyed the small sitting area that I had parked myself in, in front of the elaborate tree. And something in my stomach flushed. Heat around my waist rose up my back and prickled the hairs of my neck. I gathered my bags, my coat, and my scarf—leaving the coffee he'd bought me—and I hurried away.

The main gates were all bustling like a department store, everyone angry, negotiating, or sad, trying all of their human instincts and survival skills to get themselves out of the jam that was quite literally beyond anyone's control. Part of me wanted to announce over the intercom that there was absolutely no point and they should all just go get a snack and take a nap. But the other part of me—the one that was winning at the moment—was the part that needed to hide.

I had no direction, but it didn't matter. I followed moving walkways, escalators, and corridors away from the couch; the dark-haired, perceptive stranger; and that glittering tree. Soon enough, I was sure I had accomplished my task of hiding, because I, myself, felt lost. I had gone up at least four escalators and was fairly certain I was in a restricted area. But the lights were dim in the hallway, which led back toward the atrium that I was sure overlooked the wide-open space I had been in before. There was a cushioned bench tucked into a nook just before the hallway forked off, and I slid down onto the gray tufted cushion and wished aloud for my bed and my apartment. I tucked everything I owned between me and the wall and leaned heavily against it, reclining my head.

I wanted to cry, truth be told, even though I wasn't much of a crier. I considered the coffee cup that sat on the couch in my place, much like a glass slipper. I didn't like what I had just done. It wasn't mature, it wasn't kind, and, most of all, it was selfish—maybe even cowardly—but it had felt necessary at the time.

Chapter 4

"Ma'am?"

A timid young man's hand touched my shoulder and woke me. An *ouch* escaped my mouth as I felt the crick in my neck when I straightened up to look at him.

"Hi," I said, still wincing from the pain that groaned in my neck and along my shoulder.

"Can I help find you some accommodations?"

"No—thank you—I don't need a room." I rubbed the knot on my collar bone.

"May I see your ticket please?" He smiled at me and extended a hand.

"Oh—am I not allowed to be up here?" I asked in a surprised voice as if I hadn't already considered that I might not be. "I got a little turned around," I added, handing him my boarding passes. He quickly scanned them at a kiosk on the opposite wall.

"Looks like you've been upgraded to our elite sky crown club. If you'd like to follow me, I can get you into our sky crown suite."

"What do you mean?" I asked, continuing to sill against the wall and feeling my left eyebrow lift in dismay.

"The sky crown suite has dinner and drink service, massages, TVs, and a lovely fireplace. It's decorated quite nicely this time of year as well," he answered without missing a beat.

"No, I mean how did I get upgraded? My original ticket was coach." I wrung my hands as he beckoned me to stand and proceeded to help with my bags and coat, urging me with his hands to follow him.

"It's just what's in the system, ma'am. Right this way."

Bewildered, I followed him down the hall and to the right to two double doors of thick glass with a milky film so that one could see the warm firelight from the other side but not actually see into the room. The handles were long, straight, modern brushed nickel and had small airplanes etched into them.

The young man flashed his key card up to the panel on the wall. The door buzzed, granting access, and he ushered me in. He showed me to a tiny closet-sized room with a bed in it—somewhere between a cot and a massage table—which he explained was my own private room to store my things, take a nap, and request a massage.

"Is this for real?" I asked, feeling like I was still asleep and this was a dream.

"People usually feel that way the first time they come here," he whispered. "Even if it's a glitch, I say enjoy it—it's Christmas." He walked me by the buffet and the bar. "There's even a balcony, which is lovely in summer, but I doubt you'll want to enjoy the view tonight." He smirked at me and bowed slightly as if to excuse himself from the queen, and I had a panicked jolt that there had to be a dreadful mistake. "If you need anything, just let us know."

I gave him a timid “thank you” and a wave as he turned on his heel to leave, gathering a few discarded coffee mugs from tables as he left. *This is ludicrous. I don’t belong in here,* I thought to myself as I studied the people I saw lounging under a ball game on the oversized TV. Some were reclining together drinking whiskey in a plush corner booth. As I passed the buffet again, my stomach growled, and, seeing that no one was by the fireplace yet, I loaded my plate with Christmas-y foods and found a navy blue velvet chair that I convinced myself I could enjoy, for just a little while, even if I was an imposter.

After I had finished my sampling plate, I stared at the fireplace and mindlessly stroked the velvet on the armrest in several directions.

“May I join you?” asked a dark brown man with a white turban and a thick staccato accent as he bent over into my line of sight.

I had been in a daze, staring at the fire, but his jolly and foreign-sounding voice drew me out of my thoughts. I nodded sweetly and asked him to please help himself.

“You are find the good place, yes?” he asked with the friendliest smile I had seen all day. His dark chocolate eyes almost disappeared behind his cheeks.

“Yes. I don’t deserve such good fortune. But I am enjoying this fire,” I answered him, thinking I should get out of here before someone discovered that they had made a mistake and I was a squatter in the fancy club.

"You are missing your Christmas, are you not?" the man continued.

"Yes. But I am not too sad about that." I spoke simply to put him at ease about speaking English with me.

"Not a bad way to spend the evening. More food than we can eat. A nice fire. Friends."

"Oh. I agree. Are you traveling with friends?" I asked inquisitively. "I am here alone. If you have friends, they can join you here, and I can move...," I said, sounding more insignificant than I intended to.

"Oh, no—no—I see you. I know your meaning. I meant you and I. We shall be friends."

I squinted my eyes at him as if he couldn't possibly be serious. He didn't even know my name yet; how could he have determined to be my friend? Maybe he didn't understand the meaning or the context. Maybe I should order a massage and disappear into my closet, hibernate until spring, and come out when everyone was gone. Maybe I never should have abandoned my seat by the tree. My coffee. Maybe I never should have tried to go to Massachusetts for Christmas.

"My name is Benhami. But you can call me Ben." He rose slightly in his seat, bowed to me, and reached for my hand as I extended my own.

"My name is Blake."

"How wonderful to meet you, Blake."

"Pleasure to meet you as well, Ben."

We lounged comfortably in our chairs, warming ourselves by the fire and doing our best to content ourselves with our situation. *Stranded with strangers,* I thought. *Sounds like a good book title.*

Even though I was probably considered painfully timid by my co-workers and I rarely trusted my own voice, I knew that the best way to ease a situation with strangers was to ask questions. Research. It came like second nature to me, and, although it was the opposite of being invisible, it was the other thing I did best.

"Ben, are you on your way to home or from home?"

"I have been away for many weeks now. I am on my way home." He smiled broadly, and I knew he was wishing he was there.

"Where are you from?" I asked.

"I am certain that you have not heard of my country. But I have a very large family, and people come from all over to eat my mother's food, you know?"

I didn't, obviously, but I loved the idea of people gathering in droves, and I smiled as I asked, "What is your favorite thing she cooks?"

"Oh, my, Blake—" He said my name as an exclamation, which made me laugh through my nose as he gushed over several savory dishes I couldn't even catch the names of before settling on his favorite. "Laddoos are my favorite. They are these little round sweets. They are made from coconut and have pistachios in them and sometimes raisins. Oh, I crave them, you know?"

We laughed together as he exuded excitement as if he held an invisible sweet treat in his hand. Soon, he stood and offered to refill my plate, which I refused, but I did want a hot chocolate.

"I must have more of those pastry things," Ben said as he strode briskly away. "They are so good."

When Ben returned with his plate and my hot cup, he situated himself and turned the conversation to me before I could continue with my mental list of questions. "You will excuse me, Ms. Blake, but do you have a family?"

"Sadly, I do not."

"You are an orphan, sweet friend?"

"Oh, no," I explained hurriedly, "I have parents."

He laughed a hearty and confused laugh. "But Ms. Blake, then you have a family, have you not?"

Does seeing someone once a year make them family? I wanted to say, but I didn't.

"I supposed I do. I don't see my parents much. I just meant I do not have a husband or children."

"I see. Sometimes, family is people we choose, yes? Not so much people we share blood with." He nodded in understanding. "I have these people too."

I delighted in his sweet mannerisms and the friendly grace about him. He somehow managed to make me feel at home even though we had just met, not that I would tell him that.

“I have a sister. In my country. And she has these little boys.” He gestured to show how tall the boys were, and his face lit up. “They are wild. They are crazy. Little tyrants, you know? They drive me crazy most days—they are never quiet. They break my house. But I adore them. You know?”

I laughed again and realized how much I was enjoying myself. A spark of surprise twitched in my chest. Ben’s voice put me at ease, and his naive assumptions that I knew what he meant made me long for things I didn’t have.

He laughed and told me he could not help himself and needed another pastry. He disappeared back over to the food as I lazily leaned my head over in my hand and went back to watching the fire. I had laid a magazine in my lap but hadn’t even opened it. The cover showed a Southern front porch with Christmas topiaries and buffalo check bows on olive branch wreaths. It looked idyllic and curated; you wanted to believe that the family that lived there were just as warm and inviting as their front porch—and, of course, they were great conversationalist and made gourmet food but never let the stress of the holidays overtake the value of the people in their home.

But it was just a picture. A staged photograph of a life I, in this moment, thought maybe I wanted. Not the porch, of course. I didn’t care for the South other than their sweet tea and their smoked meats. I wanted a family. Someone I didn’t feel obligated or begrudged to see—people that filled me joy and filled my home with laughter. I was overthinking things at this point perhaps, but it was an unfortunate side effect of fire-staring. Part of me felt guilty for feeling like my parents weren't my family, but the honest part of me knew that it wasn't my fault.

"Here, Ms. Blake. Here is one of my chosen people now," Ben said, coming toward me with a full plate and pointing back toward the bar. Ben shifted his body to the right and revealed the back of a head with rich dark hair and strong shoulders.

How is he here? Seriously, what are the odds? He has to be following me, right? I scoffed at myself. *Why would he be following you, Blake?*

"Nick!" Ben called as he set his plate down and motioned eagerly toward me and Nick as if bringing us together. I definitely did not want Nick to think that I wanted that. "Come, meet my Blake."

Nick dropped his fork at my name and craned his neck to look in Ben's direction. Then, his shy smile returned, and he bent to retrieve the fork. An attendant quickly took the utensil from him, and he found a new one before hurrying over to us. *Clearly, he didn't know I was here. So, that's something.*

"Hi," Nick said cordially as he reached us. Okay, so he wasn't going to tease me or give me a hard time about running away in front of Ben.

"Hi. I promise I'm not following you," I said, unintentionally mimicking his earlier comment to me.

"No, I would never think that. One cannot follow and run away at the same time," he mumbled as he bent my way, sitting down.

My cheeks flushed, but no one seemed to notice as we settled back into our chairs.

"You two have met before?" Ben surmised.

"Just briefly," I said a little too quickly.

Ben clapped his hands together as if he was pleased. "Nick is my people. We have known for many years. We met in my country."

I nodded as if this all made sense to me and I had zero questions, but, of course, it didn't, and I did, in fact, have lots of questions. But I kept them to myself, as I did most of my thoughts.

We listened to Ben tell more stories about his wild nephews and favorite holiday foods, which did not sound nearly as appetizing to me as sweet potatoes with pecans and brown sugar. And the thought of the sweet potatoes made me want to return to the buffet, though I knew it was more likely that I was avoiding Nick than appeasing my hunger.

I surveyed the new items that the attendants had brought out, complete with pumpkin tarts and twice-baked potatoes and roasted pine nut hummus.

"I want to apologize if something I said or did made you feel uncomfortable," Nick said in a low whisper as he slid up beside me. He had just finished filling his plate, so I knew he wasn't over here for food, which caused a heat to spread up my neck and into my hairline.

Why do you keep showing up wherever I am, and why do you care? was the retort that fired off in my brain, but, instead, I smiled meekly and simply shook my head.

"No, you don't want me to apologize, or no, it wasn't something I did or said?" he asked.

"No, I don't want to have this conversation," I said flatly. I tried to make it as soft as I could, to not offend him, though I figured it was a little late for that.

"Ok." He put a hand up in surrender. The heat on my neck spread, and I put a pumpkin tart on my plate and turned away from him.

After returning to our seats, the conversation turned to Christmas traditions, mostly because Nick and Ben starting reminiscing about years they had spent, much like this one, together over a holiday. Nick didn't look my way during most of the conversation, and I felt like slinking away into my sleeping closet. Ben, though, was attentive with his eyes and his smile as he spoke.

"I don't celebrate the same holidays as Nick, but still, it felt like a family gathering anytime we would find each other like this. You know?"

I nodded once again, even though I didn't. I supposed that my job and my lifestyle kept me fairly private, and I didn't have close friends that stood in as a family substitute after I moved away from my parents. But then again, I didn't even know what to look for. Before I knew what was happening, words were coming out of my mouth, and I realized that I found it quite hard to be invisible with Ben.

"May I ask what a family gathering feels like?" I asked before I could keep it in. My face flushed again at the apples of my cheeks, and I wondered if it was visible or just internal. I hoped Nick didn't notice. Ben looked at me, puzzled, the same way he had when he'd realized I was not, in fact, an orphan, but he answered me anyway.

"Mine are loud." That made Nick laugh a little through his nose. "They are, can we say, spicy. Both as in flavorings and in personalities. We are all very different, but, when we are together, we are thankful. You know?"

No, I don't, I thought again. *And he didn't really answer the question.*

"And how does it feel when you see these people that are 'people you choose'—is that how you put it?"

"Ah, yes, I see you," he said again, and I realized he maybe meant something else, but I was not going to correct him because I loved the way he said it every time. "For example, Nick. He is special to me. He and I are very different, no?"

Nick popped an olive into his mouth and made a face that looked like he didn't disagree.

"But Nick, he listens, and he wants to understand me. He talks to me like a friend; he does not talk to me as a white man usually talks to someone different from himself—someone he needs to change. We will be friends always."

Nick nodded his head in Ben's direction as if to say thank you.

"That sounds nice," I said, ruminating on what Ben had just described. I found that my limited interaction aligned with what he had said about Nick, though I was constantly trying to avoid him.

"There's always tons of food, tons of hugging and singing, drinking and dancing. We tell old stories just to keep our facts straight, and we tell new stories to impress our wives," Ben finished, and, at that, we all laughed.

Nick had put his plate down but was still chuckling to himself as he sat back up, and we caught eyes. His laugh dissolved back into that shy smile, and I shrugged at him, smiling but still wondering what on earth I was doing here, if I had hurt his feelings, and why he cared why I had run. Ben excused himself to find the bathroom but told us to keep his seat warm.

"I thought you were going to your parents' for Christmas?" Nick inquired, clearly not upset with me.

"I was. But my childhood home and family of origin don't feel anything like that when I visit. I've always wondered what other people experience." I divulged too much and instantly regretted saying all those words.

Nick just nodded thoughtfully. "If you don't mind me asking, what does it feel like?" he pushed a little further.

Did I mind? I was skeptical of this man, even though Ben obviously trusted him with his life. Why was I so at ease with Ben, who had announced our friendship before he knew my name, but remained cynical that Nick wasn't stalking me and about to murder me in my massage room? *Not that he would want to—that seems narcissistic to think he would want to stalk me,* I reminded myself.

"Like eggshells on top of landmines," I described without really having to think about it.

Nick's eyebrows arched in surprise, but our conversation was cut short as a beautiful black women sat down on the other end of the couch Nick was on. Her sleepy child crawled up in her lap, and a blond gentleman sat down in the chair next to me. Suddenly, our private area was full, and I felt the urge to run again. Maybe I would order a massage and retire for the night. But Ben returned before I could think of an excuse.

"Ah, what providence! We have new friends."

He makes friends so easily, I thought. What if these people were, say, murderers or international thieves? Would he still just assume they could be friends?

"Thank you for letting us join you," the blond gentleman said in a strong Swedish accent. "It looked so cozy and a little bit like home. And I suspect we could all use a little bit of home right now."

"Yes, anything that feels like home," Ben chimed in. "This is our living room for tonight," he laughed, "and the finest living room I've ever been in thanks to my friend Nick, here."

"I'm Michael," said the man as he extended his hand and shook each of ours. The striking black woman with her child introduced herself as Glory, and her daughter was Giselle.

"Can I get you anything?" I asked Glory. "She is so tired. I can get you a plate or a coffee?"

"Oh, that is so kind. Thank you. We have been traveling so long."

I nodded and stood, watching the kindness in Ben's eyes smile through his cheeks.

"What can I get you?"

"Coffee would be wonderful. And just a sampling of whatever they have. I can share with Giselle."

Nick stood too. "I'll help." He followed me to the far corner of the room where the food and the coffee bar were set up.

"That was kind of you," he said, again using that brotherly tone he had when I'd played Settlers with the students. I felt a brief pang of guilt for abandoning them.

"Thanks for helping" is what came out of my mouth, though a host of other comments and questions were all on the precipice of tripping out instead. We loaded the largest plate with meats, cheeses, fruits, and danishes. Nick offered to carry the plate while I carried coffee, a juice for Giselle, and a handful of creams and sugars.

We exchanged a pleasant smile as we delivered the array to a grateful mom.

"You are so kind. Both of you. I teach my Giselle about kindness in this season of Kwanza, and it warms my heart to see it from others."

We nodded, and a warmth filled our small area that didn't originate from the hearth. Just then, an older Jewish man worked his way over to the couch, assisted by his cane. Nick jumped up so quickly I thought maybe he'd sat on something by accident.

"Please, sir, join us—take my seat," he said and helped lower older man down.

"Thank you, sir."

Nick slid down on the floor and leaned against my chair for support, drawing his arms around his knees.

Ben stood and came in front of the Jewish man, gave him a small bow, and shook his hand. "Friend, we are so glad to have you join us. We are a troop of misfits, but tonight, we are family."

The Jewish man gave a hearty laugh as he leaned deeply against the couch. "As most families are," he commented jovially.

How can such different people accept each other so easily? I wondered, remembering how hard it was for my parents to accept that I wanted a new experience, to move, to travel, to be a researcher rather than work in their family restaurant. I felt a sudden sadness wash over me as I thought through the many holidays when I'd played along, falling back into old habits and suppressing my thoughts, stifling my opinions and withholding my own stories just to blend into the floral wallpaper for a few days.

Nick asked a question that I didn't quite hear, but it launched stories for hours around our makeshift living room of dreidels and latkes, the colors of Kwanza, St. Lucia, and the meatballs.

"And, of course, the Americans, in all their freedom, can't have just one holiday—they have to have options," Ben teased, and I laughed a little because he was right. It had been at least an hour since the stories had begun, and I realized as Nick's head bobbed a little and leaned back against my chair that he had drifted off to sleep. Not wanting to disturb him, I curled farther into the velvet winged chair and relaxed into the warmth of the evening.

Chapter 5

I woke from my drowsiness to find Nick's head leaning against my knee. The joint was aching from being folded, but I wasn't sure what to do. I didn't want to risk embarrassing either of us, but neither could I just slip away. All of our friends had disappeared except for Glory and Giselle. Giselle laid sprawled out on the couch, and Glory smiled sympathetically at me. I motioned for her to come close, and she did.

"Do you not have a private closet?" I asked.

"No, they ran out."

"Please, take mine. I don't mind staying out here. You and Giselle, go get some rest."

Her eyes sparked with surprise and pleasure. "You are so kind. Again. Are you sure?"

"Of course. My bags are in there, but you can either move them or bring them out to me. I would help you, but I am a little trapped at the moment."

She smiled and lifted Giselle. "You two are a wonderful, kind, and generous couple."

My mouth fell open, and I stumbled over the consonants in my words. "Oh! No, we are not a couple."

"No?" Glory asked.

I shook my head, my cheeks flushing, and looked down at Nick's sleeping face against my knee.

"Maybe someday," Glory said, flashing me a wink before she turned to head toward the sleeping quarters.

I wondered if all our new friends had gone to their private closets to sleep and if we would all gather again in the morning. I wished to myself that we could.

"You can lay on the couch if you want." Nick's voice caused a jolt through my body. Realizing he was awake, I wondered if he had heard Glory's comment. That would probably be more mortifying than his head on my knee. But then again, he was awake, and he hadn't moved it. He reached up and squeezed my knee as if we were old friends.

"Go on," he urged as he leaned forward off my knee. I did, in fact, want to stretch out, so I did as he said. My joints and muscles thanked me as I lengthened, then stretched them on the long brown leather couch. I rolled to my stomach and folded my arms under my head as a pillow.

"Can I ask you a question?" Nick prefaced as he slid over next to the couch and leaned against it, facing the fire.

"I supposed so," I said with reserve in my voice.

"Why do you go home if home is not a place you feel you belong?"

"Whoa. Right to the quick, huh?" I laughed and pushed the hair that had fallen over my neck back behind my shoulder. "Uh...I guess it's habit. Or obligation...or maybe even fear?"

"Maybe it's the habit of being obligated out of fear," he noted.

I was stunned. Something echoed in a far chamber of my heart, and my stomach dropped out.

"I, uh, guess that sounds about right," I mumbled.

He turned his body alongside the couch and rested his arm on the cushion, close enough I could feel warmth radiate from it.

"I gather that your family events are not happy?"

"They are...cordial."

"But what would you want them to be? If you could change it?"

I lifted up on my elbows and raked my hand through my hair and stared at the fire for a moment.

"Safe," I said finally. "Enveloping. Accepting. Vibrant. Joyful."

"Your parents' house isn't safe?'

"In one sense, yes. I mean a safe space. It's not a safe place to be myself."

"And who are you?" He smiled timidly as if he'd been wanting to ask that all day and was pleased that the moment had come but didn't want to show it.

"I'm Blake. I'm a history and art research analyst. I like used book stores and traveling. I'm really not that complicated or hard to please."

"You're also beautiful and kind," he added timidly and registered my surprise. "If you don't mind me saying so."

"I probably should," I said, looking down and picking at my cuticles. "Because I don't know you. But somehow, right now, I don't."

He smiled, that timid smile that, just in the few hours we had spent together, was becoming familiar, and his hand reached out toward me—but it hesitated. I knew what he was reaching for, that stray lock that couldn't decide which side of my part it belonged on and was constantly drifting down into my eyes. He paused, just for a second. I didn't move, sort of giving him permission, and he softly tucked the strand behind my ear, leaving a trail of blush behind on my skin.

"First off," he said, "everyone should have a place to be themselves. Secondly, I think we're starting to get to know each other," he smirked, "even now."

Even now. He makes it sound like something is happening. Is something happening? If what is happening is the something I'm imagining happening, surely it doesn't happen this fast? Or at an airport. On Christmas Eve? Calm down, Blake. Nothing is happening.

"Where do you feel like yourself?" I dove headfirst in the deep end of this conversation before I had enough sense to put on an emotional flotation device.

Nick tilted his head up and scratched at the stubble on his chin, thinking. "I feel most accepted and free to be myself in the woods, with friends."

I rolled to my side and propped my head in my hand. “Why is that, because the trees can’t judge you?”

He laughed, and the small rumble in his voice and the firelight that danced in his eyes caused a strange wave of warmth down my waist where my arm was draped along my hip. He was extremely attractive up close—not that I’d been up close with very many men, but his expressive and, dare I say, forthright eyebrows were as dark as his hair and his downright unfair lashes. His nose was prominent but in a striking way.

“No, I have a group of buddies that go out whenever we can. They are some of my oldest friends. They know pretty much all the best and all the worst. They’ve stood by me, hauled my ass in when I was out of line, and gave me space to change when I need it. And in the woods, I just feel...” He paused, deliberating on his words. “Well, it’s just that, out there, none of the rest of this matters. You know? Perception, opinions, status, soap boxes, social media, rat race, religion, politics...none of it. There’s just a specific kind of... What am I looking for...?”

“Freedom?”

“Yes! I kept thinking ‘liberation,’ and that was close, but good grief, I must be tired if I can’t think of the word ‘freedom.’” He laughed again. “Freedom.”

I smiled at him through heavy lashes. The day’s and the night’s events were catching up with me, and I wanted to close my eyes, but I selfishly and surprisingly wanted Nick to still be there if I opened them again.

"I should let you sleep."

"Did you get me in here?" I asked before I could stop it. And once it had left my mouth, my eyes slid shut in exhaustion. I felt him re-tuck the strand of hair even though it didn't need it.

"Yes," he admitted in a whisper.

"I feel guilty. All those people down there."

"Why?"

I grunted a little, lifted my head off my hand, and laid down on the couch. "I'm lying on a couch in front of a fire, being treated too kindly by you. And they are all down there, uncomfortable. I don't deserve it. They..." I couldn't finish my words any more than I could open my eyes.

"Yes, you do," he whispered as Christmas Eve dissolved into dreams behind my eyelids.

Chapter 6

"No, don't wake her," I heard Ben say as I stirred, and my eyes fluttered open.

"I'm awake," I whispered groggily. "What's going on?"

"Here," Ben said, helping me sit up—not that I needed it but he was grandfatherly, and it was endearing, so I let him. He handed me a cup of coffee and sat next to me as he explained. "Nick has arranged everything. Come awake and you will see."

My back ached, and my neck had a crick in it from sleeping on a plush lounge couch that was luxurious to look at but not, apparently, made for sleeping.

But I bet it was better than the floor downstairs, I thought. I remembered what Nick had said last night about my deserving to be in here, and I couldn't make heads or tails of what that meant. My thoughts quit chasing their own tails when my eyes finally adjusted to the morning light and the new scene that Ben had woken me up for.

In the corner to our left, just past the fireplace, an enormous Christmas tree was turning lazily. It was as if the tree had been sectioned off into fourths, and as it slowly turned, I could see each new section. The first was traditional with plaid ribbon cascading from the top, red and gold ornaments accentuating the limbs on the way down. It was a fake tree, but it had been made to look as though it had a fresh coat of snow. As it slowly turned, it revealed the next section with blue velvet ribbon and paper dreidels that wound their way down the side. I stared in amazement at the expertly decorated tree, quickly catching on to the theme.

The next section was filled with cranberries and orange slices on string along with candles and dahlia horses. The final section was brighter than all the others with bold green, black, and red ribbons adorned with small fruits.

I watched the tree turn several times in amazement and then stood to inspect it closer. The detail, the thoughtfulness, and the diversity were all overwhelming.

"Nick did this, you said, Ben?"

Ben was watching me as I watched the tree, smiling. He nodded. "He made all this himself," Ben answered with pride in his voice.

"Where is he?"

"He said he had things to do. But he brought us breakfast. He will return," Ben relayed as he turned to point out a full spread on a long table that also had not been there the night before.

"I am just speechless," Glory said with a hand on her stomach. "It almost takes the sting out of not being with family, doesn't it, Ms. Blake?"

I nodded clumsily, still feeling dumbfounded by such a gesture but also because Glory's words meant nothing to me; I didn't feel such a sting to not be with my parents in their house for Christmas. I didn't feel homesick. I didn't feel nostalgic.

But *this*—this made me feel something deep in a strange and forgotten place in my stomach. And, at the moment, it echoed from its emptiness.

Maybe that's hunger, Blake, I scolded, trying to push the feeling back to the cavern from which it had come.

The elderly Jewish man toddled over to me with his cane and patted my hands as I went to shake his, realizing I hadn't properly introduced myself the night before.

"Come, my dear. It will not do to let such kindness get cold."

His sentiment warmed my chest like a sweater. He was right. Whatever Nick's motivations, it would be rude to let the breakfast go to waste. I smiled and took his arm and began to escort him to the table.

"My name is Blake, by the way. I apologize for not catching yours last night, sir."

"Oh, my dear, you are a gem. My name is Levi Cohen. But you may just call me Cohen. All my family does."

His small statement was not lost on me—*his family does*—but I didn't comment on it. "Your names are both tribes, are they not?"

"Ah! She knows my heritage. Indeed, my dear, indeed. My mother was from the tribe of Levi. And she married my father from the tribe of Cohen. They were not the first, obviously. But in our immediate families, it was a big deal. And their marriage brought a lot of unity to our tribes. Peace for generations."

"That's beautiful, Cohen. It's lovely to meet you."

"And you, my dear," he said as we sat at the table. The empty seat left next to me was not lost on me, nor were the bright, happy smiles around the table of my new friends. The fragrant coffee wafted up from French press pots in the center of the table. Plates of fruit and nuts sat next to plates of meat and potatoes with tiers of pastries on either side.

I felt at a loss for words. It was the most decadent spread I had ever seen, which probably spoke more to the sheltered life I was living in my research bubble than to the table set before us. But I couldn't imagine, for the life of me, why Nick had done this. What would make him be so inclusive of strangers? What would make him honor their diverse faiths and holidays? Did he just feel sorry for everyone? Did he have a savior complex?

As my mind was resisting all these gestures, my hand was reaching and filling my plate. The anxiety welled up in me, and, as the croissant landed on my plate and the coffee poured from the carafe, I forced myself to stand.

"Please excuse me," I said abruptly, which was met with looks of surprise and concern. But I couldn't look them in the eyes as I backed away. I turned, only to bump into the broad shoulder of the dark-haired benefactor.

Are you kidding me? I can't get away from this model of perfection.

"Everything okay?" Nick asked, almost taking my shoulders with his large hands but, at the last second, refraining.

"Yes," I said, hurrying past him before I could lose my nerve. *You're nerve for what, Blake? Running away again? It takes nerve to compulsively run? Doubt it.* "I—uh—just need to step out for a second. Call my parents," I lied.

I hurried out. I ran down the hall. I burst into the closest bathroom and locked myself in a stall. Sliding down the wall, I curled my knees up into my chest and wrapped my arms tightly around them.

What are you doing, Blake? What are you thinking? Now what? Now how are you ever going to go back in there and face those people who were so kind to you? What in the world is wrong with you? You don't even have your bags, you idiot.

My eyes stung as tears welled up, and I closed my eyes, leaning my head back, allowing them to slide down my cheeks. *How messed up are you, Blake? You ran out the only good thing you had this Christmas,* I scolded myself and then suddenly thought of Nick's touch on my cheek and ear as he'd tucked the strand of hair back last night. Was he the only good thing? Or was it room full of people? Or was it just getting stranded and not having to be home with my parents?

The thought stung as much as my salty tears did. Was I a bad daughter for not wanting to be home? Had I not been what they wanted? Was that why they had been so detached?

A knock came at the bathroom door and interrupted my downward spiral. I wiped my tears, and small footsteps followed a shy voice inside the bathroom.

"Ms. Blake?"

I opened the door to find Giselle's large brown eyes and toothless grin looking back at me as she extended my phone toward me.

"Momma said you forgot this."

My phone. Did that mean Nick believed my lie? Or that he knew I had run again?

"Thank you, Giselle."

She bobbed back and forth as if she wanted to break into a twirl. "You welcome."

I tucked my phone away in my pocket and wiped my nose with some toilet paper. Giselle plopped down next to me.

"Are you sad?"

"Oh," I sniffed, "I supposed I am."

Giselle folded and refolded her socks that had a lace ruffle on them, and it reminded me of a sailor dress I wore one year for Easter with white lace socks.

"Sometimes," she began with a whistle of air through the gap where her front teeth used to be, "when I feel sad, my mom tells to help someone."

The heat kicked on, and a burst of warm air flowed above our heads. The truth of her innocent words swirled around me just like the warm air, which had a hint of cinnamon on it. She was right.

"Thank you for bringing me my phone, Giselle. Can I walk you back to the lounge?"

She nodded and stood. We walked down the hall together and stopped at the door.

"Are you not coming in?"

I shook my head. "I need to help some people." I smiled at her and patted her head.

A toothless smile spread across her thick lips as she realized I was talking about what she had said.

"But what should I tell Mr. Nick?"

"Oh, I'm sure he won't even notice," I lied again and shooed her on. "Now, run along to your momma."

"Okay!" she said, skipping back into the lounge.

I would return. I'd come back for my bags. I would say my apologies to Ben and Cohen. But there were some things I needed to do first.

Chapter 7

"Excuse me," I said as I cleared my throat just a little, enough for the tall man in a uniform with a hefty mustache to turn around and notice me.

"Yes, miss? Can I help you?"

"Well, I just wanted to know if there was any way I could help? I know there's a ton of people stranded here on Christmas, so I just wanted to be of service, if I can."

He didn't miss a beat. "Are you a nurse or a doctor?"

I shook my head.

"A cook or a barista?"

"Sadly, no. I'm a research analyst. I don't have much to offer in the way of survival skills, I suppose."

He gave a hearty laugh. "Well, we are handing out blankets and meal vouchers. You could ride along with Martha and help hand them out?" he said, pointing toward a lady with a thick head of gray curly hair who sat facing the opposite way in the driver's seat of one of those airport trolleys. I nodded, and he walked me over and introduced me to her.

"Nice to meet you, Blake. Hop on," she said in a warm Southern drawl. "We've got ground to cover."

She turned the buggy on much like you would a golf cart, and we began to wind through the halls of the airport, stopping in areas that were thickly populated. I would hand out blankets, and Martha would explain the vouchers for the cafes and pass them out. The airport had allowed all the restaurants to serve two free meals for every passenger today since I assumed they were hoping we might be able to at least leave the airport tonight even if there were still no flights out. Where I would go was something I hadn't solved yet. And for now, it didn't matter.

I squatted down near a man about my age who was sleeping on the floor near a window and tried to drape a blanket over his shoulders, but his eyes fluttered open. His brow furrowed as he tried to adjust his eyes.

"Oh! It's you?" the man half-exclaimed and half-asked, sitting up and taking the blanket from me. It was the British man from the cafe the night before.

"Hi there. Sorry you're stuck here. We are just bringing blankets and free meal vouchers around. I didn't mean to disturb you."

"Thank you," he said and then cocked his head to the side in curiosity. "Do you work here, then?"

I smiled at him, amused that his accent made his inflection rise at the end of every sentence. "No, I just wanted to help."

"Well, from a lonely man sleeping on the floor on Christmas Day, your selflessness is a true gift. Thank you..." He left it hanging for me to finish.

"Blake," I said, realizing that my name could work for a last name and could easily confuse someone, which was fine if I didn't really want to give out my name. But something in his lanky shoulders and remembering his desperation from last night, I wanted to help him more than with just a blanket. And I didn't mind giving him my name.

"I have some friends in the Sky Lounge. If you'd like, you can take my place up there. Just tell Nick that Blake sent you."

His bright blue eyes narrowed. Though his brows were almost platinum, they were thick, and when they furrowed together, they looked even more so.

"Why would let me take your place? I'm a stranger."

I don't know; there's just something about you, I thought. And then, as if I'd just gone over a hill on a rollercoaster, the pit of my stomach dropped out as a thought occurred to me. *Maybe this is why Nick did it.*

"It's Christmas, Mr...." I left it open for him this time.

"Tyndale."

"Merry Christmas, Mr. Tyndale."

He smiled at me with disbelief in his eyes and handed back the blanket. I nodded at him as he gathered his bags.

"Top floor. Enjoy."

He tipped an imaginary hat to me. "Thank you, Ms. Blake. I am astonished. Truly."

I waved him off and turned back to my duties, feeling satisfied. But as much as I tried, a sadness followed me through the airport as we traveled from concourse to concourse, handing out blankets, smiles, and hugs to all the weary, tired, and homesick travelers.

I thought about Ben, Cohen, and Glory upstairs and wondered if they would be hurt that I had left. Or if they had even noticed. I wondered if Nick would be upset that I'd sent Tyndale in my place. *Did he sense something in me? Was that why he got me in the lounge in the first place? Was it all just Christmas spirit?* I had judged him and been skeptical of him and run out on him twice, when I, myself, expected people to understand my desire to help them by handing them something as small as a blanket.

Martha pulled the cart over. "Well, dear. I suppose we're done here," she said, hiking a leg up on the seat and turning toward me. She struck me as the kind of woman who typically had a toothpick sticking out of her mouth, didn't take crap from anyone, but was hospitable and motherly to everyone she met. Her phone rang just as her mouth opened to say something more, but she put her finger up and mouthed "hang on" and exited the cart, walking over to the window. She smiled as if she was glad to hear from this person and nodded a few times, then glanced my way and turned to the window so I lost sight of her soft silvery features.

I thought about what my mother's face looked like when she answered the phone, and I saw worry and fret instead of joy and pleasure.

Martha returned to the cart and slid in next to me.

"I've got one more deliver you can help me with."

"Alright," I said, trying my best to sound casual and not too eager even though I was considering whether I was ready to face Nick or the others just yet.

"We'll park this back at the front and take the service elevator. Hold these." She handed me a stack of blankets.

"Sure," I replied, though my response was not necessary.

"I appreciate the help, dear," she said, and I liked the way she called me "dear." "Not many people would care to lend a hand on a day like this. But it sure is a tough day to be stranded."

"You can see the weariness on everyone's faces. I'm happy to maybe help ease that a little."

"I bet you'll be happy to get out of here tonight. Maybe make it home for Christmas night at least?"

"Oh—I—uh—haven't decided what I'll do." I stumbled over the words as we got inside the elevator. Martha stacked a few more blankets on my thick stack, which blocked my view of anything other than gray wool. "How 'bout you?"

"Oh, I imagine I'll have dinner with my nephew."

"Oh, that's nice. I never had any aunts or uncles. That's nice that you're close with yours."

"Yeah. I helped raise this one after his parents, my sister and her husband, died when he was a kid."

"Oh! I'm so sorry."

“Thank you, dear. He’s a good kid,” she said as the elevator came to a stop and guided me out of the doors. We walked a few paces, and then she told me to wait as she opened a door and then took the blankets from me.

My heart fluttered.

I was back in the lounge. And Nick was standing right in front of me.

Chapter 8

"You okay?" he asked with no hint of anger, bitterness, or sarcasm.

I nodded, stunned.

"Sorry, dear. Nick here asked me to deliver you back up here once we were done."

I was the last delivery. Nicely played.

"Thanks, Aunt Martha."

"You're welcome, Nick. Need anything else?" she asked as she kissed him on the cheek.

"Nope," he answered, though his eyes were on me.

"Then, I'll see you later," she said to Nick, but she squeezed my shoulders as if it applied to me too. "Thanks for helping with the blankets, Blake."

"It was my pleasure, Martha. And it was a pleasure to meet you," I said with a flush of guilt blazing at my cheeks and up my back.

Once she had gone, my eyes had the hardest time traveling from my shoes to his face, but once I managed, a flood of quiet yet urgent questions flowed out. "Why am I up here, Nick? Why did you send for me? Why did you get me in here in the first place?" I fired my whispered confusion at him, possibly just deflecting the guilt I felt for childishly running away from every situation that overwhelmed me.

"Do I seem like a con artist?"

I laughed at that. "No."

"A liar?"

"Not really." I squinted at him, wondering what he was getting at.

"An insincere cad?"

"No."

"A pompous philanthropist?"

"No."

"Then, why can't you accept my generosity? When you yourself are willing to give it?"

He'd brought me up short. "What do you mean?"

"You're willing to give up a hotel for people who need it more, you're willing to hand out blankets to those who are stranded, and you're willing to give away your spot of luxury to someone you don't know. But you can't accept any of the same."

"Because people aren't nice to me," I blurted out forcefully. " I don't have friends that care deeply about me."

Nick took one step closer to me and took my hand. "Don't you think it's time you did, then?"

I looked awkwardly to the side. "A bunch of strangers in an airport?" I scoffed.

"What's the difference between strangers and friends?" Nick asked. He dropped my hand but escorted me back through the entryway toward the large open room with the fireplace and the tree, resting a hand at my back.

I shrugged. If it was a riddle, I didn't know the answer. If it was a saying of old, I hadn't heard it.

“The difference,” he answered his own question, “is *your* heart.”

Chapter 9

I followed Nick back into the living area of the lounge and found everyone sitting near the fireplace with coffee mugs in hand, chatting as if they were old friends and hadn't just been thrown together by a frigid force of nature less than 24 hours ago.

Gloria turned her head and reached for my hand. "Glad you have returned. We missed you."

I squeezed her hand gently and winked at Giselle's toothless grin from her momma's lap.

Ben's deep, smooth voice offered me a plate of breakfast they had saved for me.

"You all are so kind. Thank you," I managed in a sheepish voice even though I knew there was more that needed to be said. Tyndall lifted his cup to me as if to say "Cheers" and smiled a grateful smile.

"I haven't eaten either," Nick said, and his hand was at my back again. "I'll join you if you don't mind?"

I felt my whole body bristle, not at his hand, not at his invitation, and not at the thought of the spark that ignited every time he touched me, but at the foreign kindness that I encountered every time I interacted with these people and the empty and pathetic way I reacted to it.

"Why didn't you eat?" I asked as we sat down at the table where, just hours ago, the enormous Christmas brunch spread had been, now empty save for the pots of coffee and the plates that had been saved for us.

“I had some things to attend to,” he said rather vaguely as he set to unwrapping the plates from their coverings. I propped my chin in my hand and studied his face, the stubble that was now showing on his strong chin, the dark lashes that were impossible thick, and the way his mouth curved slightly at the corners when he realized I was watching him.

“The analyst has questions,” he stated and set my plate in front of me, his dark eyes landing on mine and causing that spark to ignite even without touching me.

“Who are you?” I let my amazement show in my question.

“I’m just Nick. You’re Blake. We’ve already done this part,” he smiled at me, and I knew he was being coy.

“No. Because Nick has access to things no one else does. And can create a custom Christmas for four nationalities in the crown lounge of an airport. You’re not ‘just Nick’.”

He laughed a little. “Fair enough,” he said but held my gaze and said nothing more. Pushing the plate away from me with slight irritation, I raised my eyebrows at him with a hint of rejection.

“Maybe I should go, Nick.” I stood to leave. Nick stood too and in two strides was around the table and a breath away.

“Please don’t run away anymore.”

"I'm not. Not this time. I'm just excusing myself," I said flatly as I tried to breeze past him. He caught me with one hand on my waist instinctively and quickly released me. The trail of sparks where his hand had been warmed my waist and fueled my irritation.

"Nick, I'm a researcher. I don't blindly accept anything. Maybe all these lovely people can. But I have to know facts before I accept anything."

"It's Christmas, Blake." His dark eyes brimmed with a warm plea. "There are no facts about Christmas."

"Sure there are," I said, moving away from him. "Ask any of those people in the lounge that you so thoughtfully orchestrated a custom holiday for what the facts of their holiday are, and they'll rattle off facts about dreidels and falafel, St. Lucia, St. Nicholas, and Jesus Christ. Facts, Nick."

He extended his hand again, asking permission to take mine again, but I didn't relent.

"Please, Blake. Sit. Eat with me. I promise to explain," he said, his voice warm and low and full of surrender as he motioned the extended hand toward our breakfast. I reluctantly sat back down, swallowing the urge to burst through the doors and never look back; that was ludicrous considering I couldn't leave the airport.

"Coffee?" he offered as I scooted the plate back over to me. I nodded, and he began to pour.

"My name is Nick. It's not short for anything. It really is just Nick. Martha is my aunt, and she and my uncle raised me after my parents died when I was eight. Martha and Don took over for my parents after they died, but I am the heir of my parents' fortune and legacy. Which is this airport as well as several others."

He's like an airline tycoon heir, I thought. "Your parents are *The* Harringtons? You're a Harrington?" I gawked for a moment, then remembered the plane crash, the news reports, and seeing his family in the newspaper. "I'm so sorry, Nick."

His "yes" seemed to billow between us like the aromatic steam that wafted up from our coffee. It hung in the air, heavy and rich, flavorful and full of purpose. I somehow felt smaller, even less significant, and even more like an imposter.

"I'm doing my best to inherit their legacy under the radar, building a name in association to theirs that is known for generosity and love more than just capital, investments, and profits. I travel all over the world. I work different parts of the business, and, like Ben, make friends with all kinds of people. They are strangers, but they become family."

I sipped from my coffee and popped a grape in my mouth, studying the floral pattern on the napkin that I folded and unfolded with my empty hand.

Why me? I wanted to ask but didn't, still trying to process who he was. "So, why all the elaborate Christmas charade for only a few when you have a whole airport of people that could benefit from your position and resources." My analysis came out more abrupt than I intended, and I squeezed my eyes shut, regretting the words and wishing I could hide from them or make them evaporate like the steam off my coffee.

"No, don't feel bad, Blake. That's fair. I can see how that would seem that way. Martha and Don have been working around the clock along with most every employee we have to keep everyone safe and as comfortable as we can manage. I have been at their beck and call to make sure everything is running smoothly. That's why I keep disappearing."

"We both seem to have a knack for that." I smiled and looked away from him to avoid blushing.

"Yes, I guess we do."

"But that doesn't explain the elite. Why invited only certain people to the lounge? Why go to such great lengths for some but not all? I don't want to be a part of the *chosen*—that feels gross. I appreciate your kindness, but I don't deserve it. I don't even know you. I belong with everyone else who is down there suffering."

"Blake—" He paused and reached across the table, covering my hand with his. "Ben is the president of a small country. Glory is the wife of an ambassador. Cohen is an attaché...everyone who is in here is here for their own safety. Not because they are some sort of chosen elite. They have been entrusted to my care by their governments."

My brow furrowed as I processed. I unfolded and folded the napkin again. “Then why am I here? I’m not like them. I’m a nobody.”

“I saw you in the cafe yesterday, and I just had this feeling.”

“What sort of feeling?” I squinted at him skeptically.

“I just...wanted you with me.”

And as if my brain couldn't hear what he had said, another thought registered instead, and my brows flew up my forehead. “Oh! Then I’m sorry if I compromised security by giving Tyndale my spot.”

He laughed, probably at my bypassing of his admission of feeling. “Actually, you’re instincts are keen. Tyndale is a member of the British Parliament. We’d been looking for him most of the night.”

“Oh!” I said, surprised that any instincts I had could be spot on that weren’t based on research.

Before I could say more, Nick’s phone rang, and he mouthed an apology and stepped away to answer.

I abandoned my plate, walking to the large glass wall that overlooked the snow-laden tarmac. Tiny specks of people below worked tirelessly to move paths of snow. Although the sky was beginning to clear, there was so much on the ground that, often, only their heads and shoulders and shovels showed as they dug tunnels to and from the plows. I wrapped my sweater a little tighter around my waist and hugged my arms. I didn’t know what if felt like to be wanted, and I didn't even know what the words he'd said implied.

Soon, I felt the warmth of Nick's shoulder brush up against mine as he joined me by the window.

"I have some business to attend to. I'm sorry to leave again."

"Anything I can help with? I'd rather help than just sit."

His pleasure showed in his smile, and his dark eyes sparkled in the window light, but he shook his head. "We are just working to get several diplomats out quickly now that the weather is clearing. Promise you won't run again?"

"I promise. Though I won't promise I won't want to."

He smiled, laughing to himself, and squeezing my shoulder, He hesitated as if he was considering leaning in, but the moment passed, and he walked away.

Chapter 10

“How old were you?” I asked between laughs.

“Oh, I was just a tadpole. Had to be five or so.” Ben laughed to himself. “My mother was so angry with me for eating all those rolls. She had to start completely over.” He laughed so hard tears leaked from his eyes, and he sighed, falling back against the wingback chair.

“What about you, Blake? Tell us a funny story from your holiday,” Tyndale urged across the couch from me.

The room fell silent after a few choruses of agreement. I shook my head as my neck grew warm under my turtleneck, and the heat spread up to my cheeks.

“I don’t have any.” It wasn’t as if I was being shy or resisting telling personal stories; I honestly had none.

I expected them to prod me or not believe me, teasing me to tell stories of baby Blake. But surprise in their eyes was softened by cautious yet sincere smiles.

“But I do love the Christmas parade,” I offered. “I watch it every year, without fail. Mostly alone. But it’s my favorite tradition.” I smiled at the thought of one of my only holiday joys.

Giselle agreed with me and told me all her favorite floats. Soon, the conversation moved to other topics, and I stared into the fire, wondering what simple joys like laughter and funny stories I had missed out on.

Ben leaned out over the arm of his chair and whispered toward me, “I sense that you are hidden away.” His dark eyes were wise beyond reason and kind despite the hardships of his life. He scratched at his beard, combing through it and studying me. “But it’s clear to me, my dear Blake, that you are worth knowing.”

Instant and forbidden tears brimmed my lashes, and my nose scrunched against the stinging onslaught of emotion that his words had somehow triggered.

“Oh, my dear. I have upset you?” He craned himself even farther over the side of the velvet chair and reached for my hand. I shook my head adamantly, not wanting him to take back the words I had been needing to hear, probably my whole life.

“I have not?” he whispered with worry spilling over ever vowel.

“No. I—” I wiped my tears, and he offered me a handkerchief, like I should have known he had. “You cut me to the quick, Benhami, but in the best way.”

He gave a hearty laugh and patted my hand. “If I may?” I nodded “You have a family, but you have nowhere to belong.”

Astounded, I laughed again and bowed my head as I had seen him do when reluctant to give an emphatic "yes." He bowed his head slightly in acknowledgment.

"But belonging is not always a matter of relation. It is a matter of choice. I heard you speak of your life, Blake. And I hear you say things that make it as if you have retreated into a shell—for safety."

He wasn't wrong. But suddenly, the quick I'd been cut to hurt a little more. Because it was about my choices, what I had done to continue not belonging. Hiding. Sheltering. Running. Blending in. Being invisible.

Ben tilted my chin up towards him. "I have said too much."

"No," I interrupted him. "Ben. No. I am sorry. I have just never had anyone speak straight into my soul before. You are completely right. Maybe I didn't feel wanted or accepted as a child. But I chose to not belong as an adult."

"I, for one, would gladly take you home to my family and make you one of us. But I am not sure you would like our country."

"I would love it, I am sure."

"I also know someone who would be very upset with me if I took you away."

I smirked at him and questioned him with me eyes, which made him laugh and fall back against his chair. Too embarrassed to ask any further questions, I leaned back against the couch and noticed Cohen snoring rhythmically in the other wingback chair and

Giselle sleeping in her mother's lap. Tyndale smiled at me and went back to working from his laptop.

I enjoyed the silence among friends for long minutes before I decided to try and sleep on a cot. I excused myself from those that were still awake and closed the door to the small sleeping closet. The bed was as soft as the couch, but the pillow was cloudlike, and the blanket was heavy and plush. My head pulsed from restraining my tears and then not being able too, but, as darkness enveloped me behind my eyelids, I drifted off to a dreamless sleep.

I woke to a soft rap at the door. Bleary-eyed and a tad off-balance, I sat on the edge of the bed and told whoever it was that they could come in. Nick appeared in the doorway.

"There you are."

My voice was froggy from exhaustion. "I promised not to run off."

"I'm glad you slept."

"How long have I been out?" I asked, pulling the blanket around me and motioning for him to come in, yawning.

"Couple hours," he said, sitting down next to me on the cot.

"I was talking with Ben and then was sort of on vulnerability overload and just crashed."

"I missed you being vulnerable?" he teased.

"It was unintentional, I assure you. Ben could read my soul like cards. It was intense."

"What did he say?" he asked with that shyness I had initially witnessed returning. It made me smile.

"He called me out on the fact that I try to be invisible. And he said that belonging was a choice. Well, that's the Cliff's Notes version at least."

"Ben has an incredible talent for calling you out and making you grateful for it."

I smoothed my hair, realizing I hadn't even been aware of what I looked like, waking up and letting him in. I wanted to fall in a crack in time and just be obliterated into a black hole.

"Don't worry. You look beautiful," he whispered, and I realized then that I could live off those words from him for a month. My mouth was agape, and he laughed. "I would have said something if you had drool on your face."

"Would you have?" I asked for assurance, still worried my hair looked like a bird's nest.

"Probably not," he laughed, and I shoved his shoulder with mine. "I probably would have still thought you look beautiful," he added shyly, and, before I could think it through, I threaded my fingers through his and clasped our hands together. He didn't stiffen or withdraw, and I prayed he felt sparks ignite up his palms, all the way to his chest, because that's what I felt.

He stared at our hands for a moment before he spoke again. "Do you know where you would like to belong?"

"No," I said honestly, leaving my hand where it was even though my whole body told me I was a fool for making a move like that. He probably felt trapped and didn't want to offend me. But I didn't move a muscle. "I always thought it was the other way around, ya know? Like someone else tells you that you're allowed to belong. I never thought that I got to decide. So, I guess I've never thought about it."

I shifted uncomfortably.

"And I have parents. And I feel horrible about the way I feel, considering..." I paused, not even able to bring myself to compare my situation to his. "But I do, you know. Have parents. And I grew up in a place where I was supposed to belong. Only I never felt that way."

"Why do you think that is?"

I shrugged, silently begging my whole body to not burst into tears. "I know they try, ya know? I know they do. They do the best they know how. But they don't even know me."

"Have you ever told them that you feel this way?"

"I think that's the thing. It's never been okay to be myself or have feelings. And I've always made choices they judge. I doubt it would make a difference."

He lifted our hands and gently kissed my wrist. "You deserve to feel at home. You deserve to be loved and adored."

When he lowered my hand and met my eyes again, I slowly withdrew my hand, not out of regret but out of fear that, if I didn't, I might make another move.

"Why me, Nick?" I asked again in a low voice as if I thought anyone would hear us.

"Would you believe me if I told you that I couldn't explain it?"

"No," I shook my head. "I'm a research analyst, remember? I don't believe things I can't explain."

He made a throaty noise as if he disagreed but he held the smile on his lips and shook his head. "Well, I can't, and that's the only way I know how to explain it right now."

I mimicked the noise he had made, and that made him laugh.

"C'mon. I came in here to get you. Some of the guests are leaving soon, and I had one more Christmas event planned."

Chapter 11

We stood in a circle, our little band of misfits, and held hands around the tree. Nick was on my left, and Giselle's greedy small hand was on my right. Ben sang a haunting melody that he explained was about being bliss and high praise of women.

And then, Cohen sang the staccato consonance of his Jewish hymn.

Ma-oz Tzur Y'shu-a-ti
Le-cha Na-eh L'sha-bei-ach
Ti-kon Beit T'fi-la-ti
V'sham To-da N'za-bei-ach
L'eit Ta-chin Mat-bei-ach
Mi-tzar Ha-mi-ga-bei-ach
Az Eg-mor B'shir Miz-mor
Cha-nu-kat Ha-miz-bei-ach
Az Eg-mor B'shir Miz-mor
Cha-nu-kat Ha-miz-bei-ach

Our smiles were ear to ear as little Giselle belted out the rhythmic lyrics of her homeland, and then, when she would contain herself no longer, she began to dance. We followed suit.

The quiet Swedish gentleman, Michael, said he did not sing but offered to hum a tune, and I closed my eyes as he hummed, feeling the sacred lament even though I didn't know the words.

Then, Tyndale looked to me, as did Nick, and my neck grew hot again. They did not know, but I vowed never to sing in public again when I was thirteen.

"I imagine we know some of the same?" Tyndale asked.

I nodded, though I was devising a plan to get out of this, and I knew a flush was spreading up my face, because Nick squeezed my hand.

"O Holy Night?" I asked timidly, not believing I was about to sing in front of Nick.

O holy night

The words were shaky as they left my lips, and the sound of my voice felt foreign even though it came from my mouth.

The stars are brightly shining
It is the night of
Our dear Savior's birth

Nick was looking at me, I could see from the corner of my eye, but I couldn't bear to meet his gaze. Tyndale's voice melded with mine, and my tone solidified.

Long lay the world
In sin and error pining
Till he appeared
And the soul felt its worth

As I said the words, my whole self heard them for the first time, and I felt the tear escape as I heard a third voice join mine.

A thrill of hope
The weary world rejoices
For yonder breaks

A new a glorious morn

As we went into "Fall on your knees," I found I couldn't tell where my melody ended and his harmonies began.

It was the most divine night I had experienced. These diverse souls that had come to feel like family in a matter of two days had managed to undo me. Absolutely wreck me. We sang each other's sacred songs. We learned about each other's traditions. We ate together. We'd been weary together. And, as much as I knew this carol was about Jesus Christ, it wasn't until these people had appeared that my soul had truly known its worth. Till Nick had appeared. I felt him squeeze my hand as tears rolled down my cheeks, my eyes closed, uninhibited as we finished the song.

Ben breathed heavily as if he was overcome. "That was truly holy. And beautiful."

Cohen stepped forward. "I just want to say how grateful I am to Nick for such a special space you have given up. We were stranded, but you made it home. We were strangers, but you brought us together as family. Thank you." He lifted his prayer hands to his head and bowed toward Nick. Everyone agreed in a chorus of gratitude.

"It was my honor," Nick replied. "Merry and Happy Christmas, Happy Hanukah, Happy Kwanza, St. Lucia Day," he said as he began hugging everyone. "And now, it is my pleasure to escort most of you onto a flight that will get you closer to home."

I said goodbye to Tyndale with a hug and his gratitude for all my good Samaritan-ness. I scooped up Giselle, and we hugged Glory together, promising to stay in touch. Cohen left me his address and said that he preferred handwritten letters, which I wholeheartedly agreed to. Ben wrapped me up in his broad arms.

"You have been a gift to me this holiday, Blake."

"I think it's more likely to be the opposite of that, Ben. You have opened up the shell. And I am grateful to have met you."

"We will meet again soon," he said, and I knew what he meant. I hoped so.

Nick escorted them out, and I found myself alone for a moment. I wondered to myself what coincidence had brought us all together and where to go from here. I really wanted a shower and my bed. I really wanted another nap. I also really wanted to talk to Nick.

When he returned, he found me watching the tree turn slowly, mesmerized by its odd beauty. He sat down next to me on the couch, not touching but close enough that he could if he wanted to. We sat in silence for a while, the colors on the tree starting to blur together as it turned, as if all the differences and diverse traditions no longer had boundaries and hard lines. We were all just family, celebrating. I wished that were true of my own family. I squeezed my eyes shut as I turned toward Nick, drawing my knees up on the couch between us.

"Nick..." I paused as he turned toward me, and I felt a flush on my cheeks that wasn't from the fire. "What have you done?"

"What do you mean, Blake?" He smiled at me, playing along.

"Two days ago, I was lost, in hiding, and feeling completely alone. And you managed to shake all of that up like a snow globe."

"Will it just go back to the way it was, though? Like a snow globe?"

I shook my head, propped up in my hand on the back of the couch. "No. Because I know where I want to belong. And I'm pretty sure it's going to change everything."

"Oh?" he said with intrigue is his deep eyes that crackled in the firelight and a kiss just behind his lips that I was waiting for. "And where have you decided to belong?"

"Here."

"At the airport?" he asked facetiously.

"No," I said timidly, not believe the words that were about to fall off my lips. "With you."

A satisfied smile widened his mouth, and he leaned in toward me, his breath on my cheeks, my nose, my mouth. "I was hoping you would," he said just before his lips met mine for the first time. He tasted like nutmeg, mint, and chocolate. In fact, he tasted like Christmas. His tender kiss only lasted a moment before he pulled just a breath away.

"I know it doesn't make any sense. We've only known each other for two days," he said with hesitation in his dark eyes, worried I wasn't sure. But I was.

"Well, then, we'll just have to do a lot of research." I winked at him.

He chuckled and leaned heavily against the couch—exhausted, I could tell—but he rolled his head toward me and studied my face.

"When did things change?"

I brushed his dark hair back with my fingers. "I don't know. I can't explain it." I giggled and leaned over and kissed him. This time, his hand wrapped around my waist, and he pulled me close.

Later, as we stared at the fire and the glowing tree, our heads resting against each other and slowly succumbing to drowsiness, I asked, "Can we do this every year?"

"But maybe on purpose?" he added.

"And without so much snow?" I smiled.

"Gladly. Every Year."

The end

Merry Christmas

And *a Happy New Beginning*

www.ingramcontent.com/pod-product-compliance
Lightning Source LLC
LaVergne TN
LVHW050336160826
845677LV00014B/3634
9798362982607